Who

Written and Illustrated by

DAVID SPANGLER

To Sarah and Emily, my daughters,
who are now mothers
So my storytelling goes on.

To order additional copies of this book, contact:
Xlibris
1-888-795-4274
www.Xlibris.com
Orders@Xlibris.com

WhO

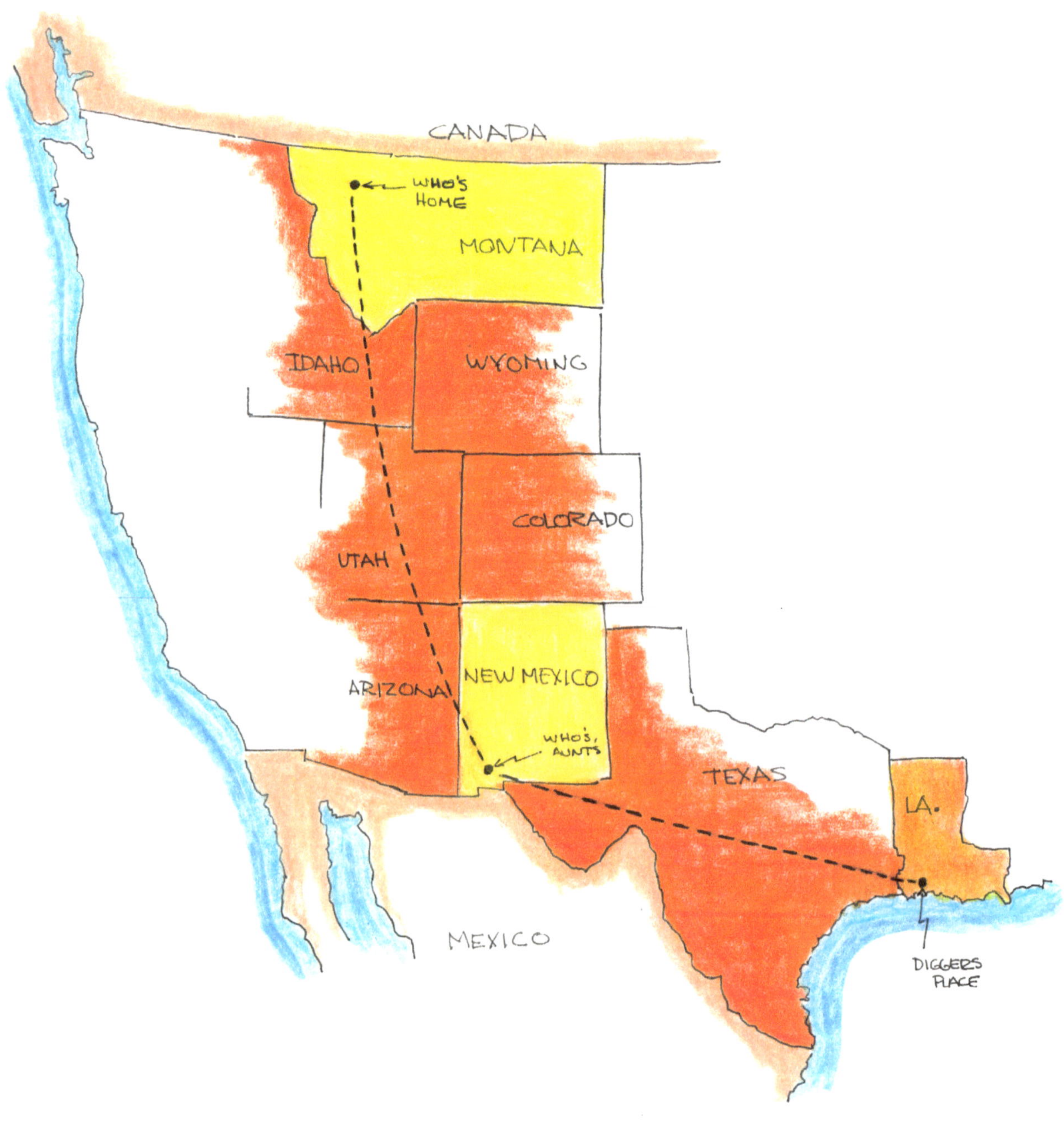

CANADA
WHO'S HOME
MONTANA
IDAHO
WYOMING
COLORADO
UTAH
NEW MEXICO
ARIZONA
WHO'S AUNTS
TEXAS
LA.
DIGGERS PLACE
MEXICO

The mountains of the Northwest are high and snow—covered much of the year. In this land lived a pair of great horned owls who had built a nest to raise a family.

Near winter's end, three eggs appeared in the nest. Their color was the same, but one egg was much smaller. The parents kept all three eggs very warm until they were ready to hatch. But they wondered who was in the small egg.

In early spring, the eggs hatched. Out came three fuzzy chicks—
two brothers and a sister. One brother was much smaller, but the
parents cared for all three of them with the same love and attention.

The young owls grew very quickly, including the smaller brother, "WHO," as he was now called. The chicks were always hungry, and it kept both parents busy feeding them. The young ones grew quickly and began to look like their mom and dad. Soon they would be ready to leave the nest.

Learning to fly was fun. It gave the three young owls a sense of freedom and excitement to see new things and to find their own food. Watching them grow and learn made the parents proud. All three young owls learned their lessons well.

In the high country, summers are short and snow can fall almost any time. WHO had grown strong and had learned his lessons well, but his size worried his parents. Perhaps he should fly someplace warm for the winter.

The idea of an adventure and becoming a "snow–bird" excited
WHO. When the cold winds began to blow, WHO knew it was time
to go. WHO's mom and dad told him to follow the bird trail in the sky.
They said, "You'll have company along the way." So off he went on his
southern trip, but the long days of flying made WHO tired.

WHO saw many new sights. After a day of travel, he sometimes found strange places to sleep.

After several days of flying south, WHO had his first stay over with a family member. He arrived at an old mission where his aunt, Sister Mary Agnes, a barn owl, lived. She welcomed him to her bell tower home. She had a gentle face and her kind words were, "Stay as long as you like."

Sister Mary Agnes shared her home with some other night animals, for she had a family of bats in her belfry. WHO also found new foods at his aunt's, such as cactus berries, tarantula spiders, and delicious snakes. What fun!

After a few days at his aunt's, it was time to fly to his cousin's, where he would be staying for the winter. His cousin, Digger, was a burrowing owl who lived near some salty water we call the Gulf of Mexico. On a cool November evening, WHO bid his aunt good—bye. He promised to stop in the spring on his return home.

WHO noticed changes during the several days it took to travel to Digger's. The air got warmer and more humid, and there was the sweet smell of flowers and fruits. Near the shore, WHO looked for Digger in a strange groups of trees, which were called live oaks.

WHO found his cousin, and the two young owls greeted each other with strange looks. WHO noticed that his cousin, Digger, was just his size. "I'm not so small after all," thought WHO.

Digger showed him his home at the base of a live oak tree. A home in the ground might be great for a burrowing owl, but not a great horned owl like WHO. WHO asked his cousin, "Would it be all right for me to live upstairs?" A quick yes was the reply.

The branches with moss and ferns made a great home. The view looking out over the water was an added bonus. What a great winter home! At night, WHO was wakened when Digger made a hissing noise like a rattlesnake, a sound WHO knew. "It's a burrowing owl's protective sound," Digger explained.

Exploring the new area with Digger was fun. WHO liked the warm sun and the salty breeze. It was so different from his home in the Northwest. He was introduced to many new foods. He really liked the clams, the fish that washed up on shore, and the many different kinds of crabs.

Winter passed quickly for WHO, and he knew it would soon be time to head north. It would be great to see his family and share his adventures with them. He bid farewell to Digger saying, "I'll come again when the cold winds blow up north." It was time to follow the trail in the sky. On his way, he stopped to see Sister Mary Agnes for a rest in her belfry. WHO told her his stories and saw the desert in its beautiful spring bloom.

His travels from his aunt's home crossed familiar territory, but the fall colors he saw on his way south were now the bright, fresh colors of spring. On his final day of travel, he saw the familiar mountains of home.

WHO was now an adult, although he was still smaller than his family. His adventures had made him strong and wise. When he saw the spire of the old tree and its nest, he knew that he was home.

The reunion with his family was joyous. They shared tales of their time apart. The love of his family made WHO realize that there's no place like home.